D0879885

JORGE AMADO, the son of a cocoa planter, was born in 1912 in Ilhéus, the provincial capital of the state of Bahia, Brazil, whose society he portrays in such acclaimed novels as *Gabriela, Clove and Cinnamon; Dona Flor and Her Two Husbands;* and *Tereza Batista: Home from the Wars.* The theme of class struggle dominates his novels of the thirties and forties, but with the fifties and *Gabriela, Clove and Cinnamon* (1958), the political emphasis gives way to a lighter, more novelistic approach. In this novel, published in the United States and some fourteen other countries, Amado first explored the rich literary vein pursued in *Dona Flor and Her Two Husbands,* basis of the highly successful film and Broadway musical. Other Jorge Amado novels translated into English and published in Avon Books editions include *Shepherds of the Night, Tent of Miracles, Tieta, Home Is the Sailor, The Violent Land,* and *Captains of the Sands.* Amado's most recent novel is *Showdown.*

THE TWO DEATHS OF QUINCAS WATERYELL

JORGE AMADO

TRANSLATED FROM THE PORTUGUESE BY
BARBARA SHELBY

Illustrations by Emil Antonucci

AVON BOOKS  NEW YORK

Originally published in Portuguese by Livraria Martins Editôra as "A morte e a morte de Quincas Berro Dágua," included in the volume entitled *Os Velhos Marinheiros*. Copyright © 1961 by Jorge Amado.

AVON BOOKS
A division of
The Hearst Corporation
105 Madison Avenue
New York, New York 10016

First Avon Books Trade Printing: December 1988
First Avon Books Mass Market Printing: April 1980

AVON TRADEMARK REG. U.S. PAT. OFF. AND IN OTHER COUNTRIES, MARCA REGISTRADA, HECHO EN U.S.A.

Printed in the U.S.A.

OPM 10 9 8 7 6 5 4 3 2 1

For

LAÍS and RUI ANTUNES,

in whose fraternal house in Pernambuco

Quincas and his folk

grew in the warmth of friendship.

"EVERYBODY LOOK OUT

FOR HIS OWN FUNERAL;

NOTHING'S IMPOSSIBLE."

(Last words of Quincas Wateryell,
according to Quitéria who was next to him)

THE TWO DEATHS OF
QUINCAS WATERYELL

I

A certain amount of confusion about the death of Quincas Wateryell persists even today. There are doubts to be explained away, ridiculous details, contradictory testimony from witnesses, divers gaps in the story. Time, place, and last words are uncertain. The family, backed up by neighbors and acquaintances, sticks to its version of a quiet death in the morning—with no witnesses, no fuss, and no last words—occurring almost twenty hours before that other, notorious death just before dawn, when the moon faded into the ocean and mysterious things took place on the docks of Bahia. Quincas's last words were sworn to nevertheless by reliable witnesses and passed on by word of mouth through steep streets and back alleys, and they meant far more to those who repeated them than a mere farewell to the world. They were a prophetic pronouncement, a message of deep significance (as one of our young contemporary authors would put it).

With so many reliable witnesses around—including Cap'n Manuel and Wide-Eyed Quitéria, a woman of her word—there are still those who deny any and all authenticity not only to the much-admired last words but also to everything that happened on that memorable night when, at an uncertain hour and in ambiguous circumstances, Quincas Wateryell dived into the gulf of Bahia and set off on his last journey, never to return. That's the world for you—swarming with doubters and skeptics who are yoked like oxen to law and order, due process, and notarized documents. These good people triumphantly display the death certificate signed by the doctor just before noon, and with that one scrap of paper—for no other reason than that it has printing and stamps on it—try to blot out the last few hours lived so intensely by Quincas Wateryell before he departed of his own free will, or so he proclaimed loud and clear to his friends and the others who were present.

The dead man's family—his respectable daughter and conventional son-in-law, a civil servant with a promising career; Aunt Marocas and her younger brother, a businessman with a modest bank account —stoutly asserts that the whole story is nothing but a gross falsehood concocted by inveterate drunkards, scoundrels on the fringes of lawful society, crooks who ought to be seeing the world from behind bars instead of enjoying the free run of the streets, the port of Bahia, the white sandy beaches, the vast friendly night. They unjustly lay at the door of these pals of Quincas all responsibility for the ill-fated life he had been leading during the past few years, to the grief and shame of his family. In fact, his name was never uttered and his deeds never were mentioned in the presence of the innocent children. As far as they were concerned, their Grandfather Joaquim, of fond memory, had decently passed away long ago, esteemed and respected by all who knew him. All of which leads us to deduce a first death, moral if not physical, dating from years back and bringing the total to three—thus making Quincas a record-holder for dying, and justifying us in thinking that the events that took place afterward, from the signing of the death certificate to his dive into the ocean, were a farce acted out with the sole aim of mortifying his relatives one last time by turning their lives upside down, covering them with shame, and exposing them to malicious gossip. He was not a man to earn respect or keep up appearances, in spite of his gambling partners' respect for the lucky gambler and the fine-talking tippler.

I honestly don't know whether the mystery of Quincas Wateryell's death (or deaths) can ever be cleared up. But I am going to try my best, for as Quincas said himself, the important thing is to attempt even the impossible.

II

In the opinion of the family, the rapscallions who reported Quincas's last moments in the streets and alleys, in front of the Trade Mart and in the open-air market of Água dos Meninos,* showed an appalling lack of respect for the dead. Furthermore, a leaflet containing doggerel verses composed by Cuica de Santo Amaro, the improviser, was enjoying a brisk sale. A dead man's memory is, as we all know, sacred and not meant to be bandied about in the dirty mouths of drunken sots, gamblers, and marijuana smugglers. Nor should it be turned into a subject for uninspired rhyming by folk singers at the entrance to the Lacerda Elevator, where so many of the best people pass by every day, including co-workers of Leonardo Barreto, Quincas's humiliated son-in-law. When a man dies, he is automatically restored to genuine respectability, no matter what sort of folly he may have indulged in when he was alive. Death wipes out the

* Salvador's most famous open-air market for generations, the Feira Água dos Meninos, was totally destroyed by fire in 1964.

black marks of the past with an absentminded hand, and the memory of the dear departed shines flawless as a diamond. This at any rate was the family's theory, and it was applauded by their friends and neighbors. According to this theory, Quincas Water-yell, when he died, became once again the former respectable, well-born Joaquim Soares da Cunha, exemplary employee of the State Rent Board, with his measured step, his close-shaved beard, his black alpaca coat, and his briefcase under his arm; listened to respectfully by the neighbors when he chose to express his opinions on weather and politics; never seen in a bar; a temperate, home-loving drinker. The family had in fact, by dint of extremely praiseworthy efforts, succeeded in making Quincas's memory shine unimpaired for several years after declaring him dead to society. They spoke of him in the past tense when obliged by circumstances to speak of him at all. Unfortunately, every so often a neighbor, or some colleague of Leonardo, or a busybody friend of Vanda (the disgraced daughter), ran into Quincas or heard about him from someone else. Then it was as though the dead man had risen from his grave to defile his own memory—lying dead drunk in broad daylight in the marketplace; or, dirty and disheveled, hunched over a pack of greasy cards in the courtyard of the Church of the Pillar; or even singing in a hoarse voice in São Miguel Alley, chummily embracing Negro and mulatto women of doubtful virtue. It was simply dreadful!

When at last, on that particular morning, a man who sold religious articles on Tabuão Street hurried in distress to the Barretos' house, which was small but neat, and told daughter Vanda and son-in-law Leonardo that Quincas had definitely departed this life in the wretched pigsty he had been occupying, the couple let out a simultaneous sigh of relief. Never again would the memory of the retired employee of the State Rent Board be dragged in the mud by the wild, thoughtless behavior of the bum he had turned into at the end of his life. Their well-earned rest had come at last. Now they could talk freely about Joaquim Soares da Cunha, praise his conduct as an employee, as a husband and father, and as a citizen, point out his virtues as an example to the children, and teach them to honor their grandfather's memory without fear of contradiction.

The saint-seller, a skinny old man with a white woolly pate, expatiated on details of his story: a Negro woman who sold cornmeal mush, beancakes wrapped in banana leaves, and other delicacies, had had an important matter to bring up with Quincas that morning. He had promised to get hold of certain herbs for her that were hard to find but absolutely necessary for her voodoo devotions. She had come for the herbs; she just had to have them; the time for Xangô's sacred rites was at hand. The door of his room at the top of the steep flight of stairs was open as usual; Quincas had lost the big hundred-year-old key a long time before. It was believed that he had actually sold it to some tourists on a lean day when he had had no luck at cards, adding into the bargain a grand story, lavishly embellished with dates and details, of its being a blessed church key. The Negro woman called, got no answer, thought he was still asleep, and pushed the door open. The sheet black with dirt, a torn bed-spread over his legs, Quincas was lying on the cot and smiling his usual welcoming smile. She didn't notice anything wrong. When she asked him about the herbs, he smiled and didn't answer. His right big toe stuck out through a hole in his sock, and his shabby shoes were on the floor. The woman, who knew Quincas well and was used to his jokes, sat down on the bed and told him she was in a hurry. She was surprised that he didn't put out his shameless hand, which never missed a chance to pinch and feel around. She had another look at his right big toe; it looked funny. She touched Quincas's body, jumped up in alarm, and felt his cold hand. Then she ran down the stairs and spread the news.

Daughter and son-in-law listened without relish to this detailed narration of Negro women and herbs, voodoo, and feeling around. They shook their heads impatiently, trying to get him to cut it short; but the saint-seller was a deliberate man and liked to tell a story with all the details. He was the only one who knew about Quincas's relatives, whose identity had been revealed one night during a monumental binge; that was why he had come. He composed his face into a suitably contrite expression to present "his heartfelt condolences."

It was time for Leonardo to go to work. He said to his wife: "You go on, I'll stop at the office. I have to sign in and explain to the boss."

They told the saint-seller to come in and showed him to a chair in the living room. Vanda went to change her clothes, and the old man told Leonardo about Quincas, about how there wasn't anybody on Tabuão Street who didn't like him. Why had a man from a good background, a man of means (the saint-seller could see he had been one, now that he had had the pleasure of making the acquaintance of his daughter and son-in-law), decided to live the life of a tramp? Had something happened at home to make him unhappy? That must be it. Maybe his wife had put horns on him; that happened pretty often. The saint-seller placed his forefingers on his forehead in sly interrogation. Had he guessed right?

"Dona Otacília, my mother-in-law, was a saintly woman!"

The saint-seller scratched his chin: why had he done it then? But instead of replying, Leonardo got up to join Vanda, who was calling him from the bedroom.

"We'll have to let people know."

"Let who know? What for?"

"Aunt Marocas and Uncle Eduardo and the neighbors. We'll have to invite them to the funeral."

"Why should we tell the neighbors right away? We can tell them later. Otherwise they'll talk their damned heads off."

"But what about Aunt Marocas?"

"I'll talk to her and Eduardo after I stop by the office. Hurry up. Otherwise that old guy'll be running around telling everybody he sees."

"Who would ever have thought he would die that way, all alone?"

"It was his own fault, the crazy screwball."

In the living room, the saint-seller was admiring a colored portrait of Quincas painted about ten years before. It showed him as a fine-looking gentleman with a high collar, a black necktie, pointed mustaches, slicked-down hair, and rosy cheeks. Next to him in an identical frame was Dona Otacília in a black lace dress, her eyes accusing, her mouth hard. The saint-seller examined her sour visage.

"She doesn't have a husband-cheating face, but she sure looks like a hard bone to gnaw on . . . saintly woman, my foot!"

III

Only a few friends from Tabuão Street were keeping Quincas's body company when Vanda entered the room. The saint-seller explained to them in a low voice: "That's his daughter. And he had a son-in-law and a brother and sister, too, all high-class people. The son-in-law's a clerk and lives in Itapagipe, in a very fine house."

They made way for Vanda to pass, waiting expectantly for her to fling herself on the corpse and embrace it, to dissolve into tears, or to burst out sobbing. Quincas Wateryell, lying on the cot in his patched old trousers, tattered shirt, and enormous greasy vest, smiled as though enjoying himself hugely. Vanda stood stock still and stared at his unshaved face and dirty hands, and at the big toe sticking out through the hole in his sock. She had no tears left to shed, no sobs to fill the room with. All her tears and sobs had been used up long ago, when she had tried again and again to persuade Quincas to come back to the home he had abandoned. Now she could only stare at him, her face flushed with shame.

He made a most unpresentable corpse—the corpse of a bum who had died accidentally and indecently, laughing cynically at her, and no doubt at Leonardo and the rest of the family. That corpse belonged in a morgue; it should have been dumped into a police wagon to be cut up by the medical students and buried in a shallow grave, with no cross and no inscription. It was the body of Quincas Wateryell, rum-swiller, debauchee, and gambler, who had no family, no home, no flowers, and no one to pray for him. It was certainly not Joaquim Soares da Cunha, respectable functionary of the State Rent Board who had retired after twenty-five years of loyal service, or the model husband to whom people had tipped their hats and whose hand everyone had been proud to shake. How could a fifty-year-old man leave his home, his family, his lifelong habits, and his old acquaintances to wander the streets, drink in cheap bars, visit whorehouses, go around dirty and unshaved, live in a filthy hole in the worst part of town, and sleep on an old cot that was falling to pieces? Vanda racked her brains for a valid explanation. Often at night, after Otacília's death (not even on that solemn occasion had Quincas consented to return to the fold), she had talked it over with her husband. He wasn't crazy, at least not crazy enough to be put away; the doctors had been unanimous on that point. How on earth, then, could such behavior be accounted for?

**HE MADE A MOST UNPRESENTABLE CORPSE—
THE CORPSE OF A BUM . . .
LAUGHING CYNICALLY AT HER. . . .**

Now it was all over at last—the nightmare that had dragged on for years, the blot on the family escutcheon. Vanda had inherited a good deal of her mother's practical common sense and was capable of making rapid decisions and carrying them out. As she gazed at the dead man, a disgusting caricature of what her father had been, she made up her mind what to do. First she would call in a doctor to write out the death certificate. Then she would have him dressed in decent clothes, take him home, and bury him next to Otacília. It would have to be a very modest funeral—times were hard—but good enough so they would not lose face in the eyes of their friends and neighbors and Leonardo's colleagues. Aunt Marocas and Uncle Eduardo would help. At this thought, Vanda, her eyes fixed on Quincas's smiling face, wondered what would become of the money from her father's retirement fund. Would they inherit it, or would they get only the life insurance? Maybe Leonardo would know.

She turned to the curious eyes gazing at her. It was that scruffy riffraff from Tabuão Street whose company Quincas had enjoyed so much. What on earth were they doing there? Didn't they realize that when Quincas Wateryell had breathed his last, that had been the end of him? That Quincas Wateryell had been an invention of the devil, a bad dream, a nightmare? Joaquim Soares da Cunha would come back now and stay for a little while with his own people in the comfort of a decent house, his respectability restored. It was time for him to come home. And this time Quincas couldn't laugh at his daughter and son-in-law, tell them to go jump in the lake, wave them an ironic farewell, and walk out whistling. He was lying on the cot, not making a move. Quincas Wateryell was gone for good.

Vanda lifted her head, scanned the faces before her defiantly, and gave an order in Otacília's voice: "Do you want anything? If not, you can leave." Then she addressed the saint-seller: "Would you kindly call a doctor to sign the death certificate?"

The saint-seller nodded, impressed; and the others filed slowly out. Vanda remained alone with the corpse. Quincas Wateryell was smiling, and his big right toe seemed to grow bigger through the hole in his sock.

IV

Vanda looked around for a place to sit down. Besides the cot itself, there was only an empty kerosene drum. She stood it on end, blew off the dust, and sat down. How long would it take the doctor and Leonardo to get there? She could picture her overcautious husband at the office, explaining his father-in-law's unexpected decease to the boss, who had known Joaquim at the Rent Board in better times. But then, who hadn't known and respected him in those days? Who would ever have dreamed that he would come to such a disgraceful end? Leonardo must be having a hard time, talking to the boss about the old man's crazy ways and trying to explain why he had acted the way he had. It would be even worse if the news were whispered around the office from desk to desk, accompanied by the inevitable rude jokes, malicious snickers, and remarks in bad taste. He had been a real cross to bear, that father of hers; he had made martyrs of them all. But now they had reached the top of the hill, if they could just hold on and be patient a little longer. Vanda glanced at the dead man out of the corner of her eye. He was actually smirking—obviously he thought it was all a huge joke.

It is undoubtedly sinful to harbor thoughts of anger against a dead man, and the sin is even worse when the man was one's own father. Vanda tried to curb her sinful thoughts. She was a religious person, a regular worshipper at the Church of the Bonfim, and something of a spiritualist as well; she believed in reincarnation, for instance. Besides, Quincas's smile made no difference now. She had the upper hand at last, and before very long he would again become the peaceful, irreproachable citizen, Joaquim Soares da Cunha.

The saint-seller came in with the doctor, a young lad who was almost certainly a recent graduate, as he still took the trouble to assume an air of professional competence. The saint-seller pointed to the body, and the doctor introduced himself to Vanda and opened his shiny leather bag. Vanda got up, pushing away the oil drum.

"What did he die of?"

It was the saint-seller who explained: "They found him dead, just the way he is now."

"Did he suffer from any sort of illness?"

"That I couldn't say, Doctor. I've known him for ten years and he always seemed as strong as an ox. Unless you. . . ."

"Unless I what?"

"Unless you call rum a disease. He drank plenty of it, that's for sure."

Vanda coughed reproachfully. The doctor addressed her: "Did he work for you, ma'am?"

There was a short, heavy silence. In a faint voice she replied: "He was my father."

The doctor was young and inexperienced in life's ways. His eyes took in Vanda's neatness and cleanliness, her dressy clothes, her high heels. He peered at the dead man, so excessively poor in a room so excessively dirty.

"But did he live here?"

"We tried every way we could to get him to come home. He was . . ."

"Crazy?"

Vanda flung out her arms helplessly, close to tears. The doctor did not insist. He sat down on the edge of the bed and began the examination. Raising his head, he remarked: "Hey, he's laughing. Making fun of us."

Vanda closed her eyes, her hands clenched, her face red with shame.

V

The family council—a brief one—was held at a restaurant table in Shoemaker's Lane, across the street from a movie house. Cheerful crowds hurried to and fro as the family deliberated. The corpse had been confided to the care of a funeral parlor owned by a friend of Uncle Eduardo who had consented to give them a discount of twenty per cent. As Eduardo explained: "The coffin's the expensive part. And the cars, if the procession's any size at all. It costs a fortune. You can't even die these days."

In a nearby store they had bought new black clothes (the cloth wasn't that good, but, as Eduardo had said, it was more than good enough for the worms to chew on), a pair of black shoes, a white shirt, a necktie, and a pair of socks. Underwear wasn't necessary. Eduardo noted down each separate item. He knew how to economize, and his grocery store was doing well.

Quincas Wateryell's metamorphosis back into Joaquim Soares da Cunha was taking place under the skillful hands of the morticians as his relatives

ate their fish dinner in the restaurant and argued
about the funeral. Actually, the only real argument
was about where Joaquim should be laid out.

Vanda was determined to hold the wake in the
parlor and serve coffee, liqueurs, and cupcakes all
night. They would call in Father Roque to pray over
the body, and the funeral would take place early in
the morning so that a lot of people could come:
Leonardo's friends at work, old acquaintances, and
friends of the family. Leonardo was opposed to all
this. Why have the body brought home at all? Why
invite friends and neighbors and bother a lot of people
for nothing? It would only remind them of the dead
man's folly and unearth memories of the awful life
the old reprobate had been leading. That was just
what had happened in the office that morning—no
one had talked about anything else. Everyone there
knew some story about Quincas and had told it, accompanied by guffaws. He, Leonardo, had never
dreamed that his father-in-law had pulled so many
wild stunts. It was enough to make your hair stand
on end. And besides, a lot of people thought that
Quincas was dead and buried or living in the interior
of the state. And what about the children? They had
been taught to venerate the memory of an exemplary
grandfather resting in God's holy peace, and all of a
sudden their parents would turn up with a bum's
cadaver and stick it right under their innocent noses.

Not to mention all the fuss and commotion and the extra expense—as though the funeral, the new clothes, and the shoes weren't enough. He, Leonardo, needed new shoes himself, but he had had a decrepit old pair half-soled to save money. And now, after all this wasteful spending, when could he even think about new shoes?

Plump Aunt Marocas, smacking her lips over the restaurant's fish plate, agreed with him: "The best plan is to spread the word around that he died some-where in the interior—that we got a telegram. Then we can send out invitations for the seventh-day Mass. Whoever wants to can go, and we won't have to furnish transportation."

Vanda suspended her fork halfway to her mouth: "After all, he was my father. I don't want him buried like a bum. How would you like it if it were your father, Leonardo?"

Uncle Eduardo was not inclined to be sentimental. "If he wasn't a bum, what was he? One of the worst in Bahia. I can't deny that, even if he was my brother."

Aunt Marocas belched, from a full stomach and a full heart: "Poor Joaquim, he was so good-natured. He never did anything just to be mean. He was born for that kind of a life; he couldn't help it. One time— do you remember, Eduardo?—he tried to run away with a circus. What a hiding he got!" She tapped

Vanda's thigh as though excusing herself for what she was about to say. "And your mother, honey, was as bossy as she could be. One day he just up and left. He told me he wanted to be as free as a bird. He was a funny man, and that's the truth."

None of the others saw anything funny about it. Vanda's expression set into a stubborn frown. "I'm not sticking up for him. He led my mother and me a hard life, and mother was a good woman. It was hard on Leonardo, too. But even so, I won't have him buried like a stray dog. What would people say when they found out? Before he lost his good sense, everybody thought a lot of him. He ought to have a proper burial."

Leonardo looked at her pleadingly. He knew it was no use arguing with Vanda; she always got her own way in the end. That was the way it had been with Joaquim and Otacília, except that one fine day Joaquim had said to hell with it and walked out. Well, there was no help for it; he'd have to lug the corpse home, go out and tell friends and acquaintances all about it, call people up and invite them over, spend a sleepless night listening to stories about Quincas, with their accompaniment of sly, smothered laughter and winks of the eye—and all of this would go on until the funeral party left. That father-in-law of his had caused him all kinds of grief—ruined his whole life, in fact. Leonardo had lived in fear of "another one of the old man's stunts." Every time he opened a newspaper, he was afraid of coming across the news that Quincas had been arrested for vagrancy, as had indeed happened once. He couldn't bear to recall that day when, urged on by Vanda, he had tramped from one police station to another until he had found Quincas in the cellar of the municipal jail, barefoot and in his underwear, calmly playing poker with thieves and swindlers. And after all he had gone through, just when he was thinking he could finally breathe easy again, he had to put up with that damned corpse for a whole day and night in his own living room.

Eduardo disagreed too; and the grocer's opinion carried some weight, because he had agreed to go halves on the funeral expenses. "That's all very well, Vanda. Let him be buried like a Christian, with a priest and new clothes and a wreath. He didn't deserve any of it, but after all, he's your father and my brother. That part of it's all right. But why lay him out in your house? . . ."

"Yes, why?" Leonardo echoed.

". . . bother a lot of people for no good reason, and have to rent six or eight cars for the procession? Do you have any idea how much each one'll cost? And how much it'll cost to take the body from Tabuão to Itapagipe? A fortune. Why can't the funeral procession leave from here? We'll be the only ones in it, so one car's all we'll need. And then, if you really want to, we can send out invitations to the seventh-day Mass."

"Tell people he died in the interior." Aunt Marocas clung to her idea.

"Maybe we could. Why not?"

"Then who'll come to the wake?"

"Just us. Why invite anyone else?"

Vanda finally gave in. After all, she admitted to herself, the idea of taking the body home was a bit extravagant. It would only mean more work, worry, and expense. The best thing was to bury Quincas as discreetly as possible, tell their friends later, and invite them to the seventh-day Mass.

And so it was agreed. Dessert was ordered while a nearby loudspeaker blared forth the enticements of a sales plan offered by a local real-estate agency.

VI

Uncle Eduardo had gone back to the store, not wanting to leave it at the mercy of his thieving clerks. Aunt Marocas had promised to come back for the wake, but first she had to go home; she had left everything topsy-turvy when she had heard the news. Leonardo, at Vanda's suggestion, would take advantage of his free afternoon to stop by the real-estate agency and settle the business of a piece of land they were buying in installments. Some day, God willing, they would have their own home.

They had set up shifts for the wake: Vanda and Marocas in the afternoon, Leonardo and Uncle Eduardo that night. Tabuão Street was no place for a lady to be seen at night: it had a bad reputation and was frequented by idlers and prostitutes. The next day the whole family would meet for the funeral.

Thus it happened that Vanda found herself alone with her father's corpse that afternoon. The sounds of the poor but intense life being lived in the streets below came only faintly to the third floor of the

squalid building where Quincas reposed after the
fatigue of having his clothes changed.

The competent, well-trained morticians had done
a good job. As the saint-seller, looking in for a moment to see how things were progressing, had
remarked; "You wouldn't take him for the same
corpse."

Combed, clean-shaved, dressed in black, with his
white shirt, necktie, and shiny shoes, it was unde-
niably Joaquim Soares da Cunha who was resting in
the casket—a casket fit for a king, Vanda observed
with satisfaction, with its gold handles and ruffles
around the edges. A rough table had been im-
provised out of boards and wooden tripods, and on
it the coffin loomed, noble and severe. Two enormous
candles—high altar candles, Vanda noted with pride
—emitted a feeble flame that was barely able to hold
its own against the dazzling sunshine of Bahia. So
much sunlight, such cheerful brightness, seemed to
Vanda a lack of consideration for the dead man, besides making the candles useless and taking away
their august brilliance. For a moment she thought
of blowing them out to economize. But as the under-
taker would certainly charge the same whether they
burned two candles or ten, she decided to close the
window instead. The holy flames leaped like tongues
of fire in the dimness. Vanda sat down on the chair
provided by the saint-seller, feeling an emotion that

was not mere satisfaction at having done her filial duty, but something much deeper.

She heaved a sigh of contentment as she smoothed her brown hair. She felt as though she had finally tamed Quincas and put the reins on him again—the reins he had torn from Otacília's strong hands as he had laughed in her face. The shadow of a smile appeared on Vanda's lips, which would have been beautiful and desirable if it had not been for a certain unyielding hardness in their expression. She felt avenged for all the suffering and humiliation that Quincas had inflicted on the family, especially on her and Otacília, for so many years. Yes, Joaquim had led that ridiculous life for ten long years. "Vagabond king of Bahia," they had called him in the police columns of the newspapers. He was the sort of street character quoted by columnists avid for the facile and the picturesque. He had gone on that way for ten years, shaming the family and spattering its name with the mud of his inexcusable notoriety. "Champion rum-drinker of Salvador . . . tattered philosopher of the marketplace . . . senator of the honky-tonks . . . Quincas Wateryell, loafer par excellence"—that's how the newspapers had described him whenever his disgraceful photograph had been printed. Lord! what a poor daughter goes through in this world when she has to carry the heavy cross of a father with no sense of duty.

But now she was contented as she gazed at the corpse in its fancy coffin, dressed in a black suit, hands crossed on breast in an attitude of devout contrition. The candle flames leaped higher and made the new shoes shine. Everything was decent except the room itself, of course. That was a consolation to someone who had worried and fretted so much. Vanda thought that Otacília must be feeling happy in whatever distant circle of the universe she was inhabiting at that moment. Her orders had finally been carried out; her devoted daughter had brought back Joaquim Soares da Cunha, that good, timid, obedient husband and father who used to turn meek and conciliatory if she so much as frowned and raised her voice. There he was, his hands crossed virtuously on his bosom. The "vagabond king of the honky-tonks" and "patriarch of the prostitutes" was gone for good.

What a pity he was dead and could not see himself in the mirror. What a pity he could not be a witness to the triumph of his daughter and the rest of his worthy, outraged family!

In that moment of deep satisfaction and sheer triumph, Vanda wanted to be generous and good. She wanted to forget the last ten years, as though the competent undertakers had wiped them away with the wet, soapy rag with which they had wiped the dirt from Quincas's body. She would recall only her childhood, her adolescence, her engagement, her marriage, and the meek figure of Joaquim Soares da Cunha, who had been fond of reading the paper while half-hidden in a lawn chair, only to start up guiltily when Otacília's voice called out reprimandingly: "Quincas!"

That was the way she liked to remember him. She could have tender feelings toward that father and miss him; with a little more effort, her heart would be really touched and she could feel the emotions of an unhappy, abandoned orphan.

The room became hotter and hotter. With the window closed, the sea breeze could find no place to enter. Vanda didn't want it to. The sea, the breeze, the harbor, the steep streets running up the mountain, and their characteristic sounds were all part of that damnable folly which was past history now. Here there was room only for her and her dead father, the late lamented Joaquim Soares da Cunha, and the few cherished memories he had left her. She searched her memory for scenes long forgotten. There was the time her father had taken her to ride on a merry-go-round in Ribeira when there had been a feast-day celebration at the Church of the Bonfim. She had never seen him in such a good humor before or since—that big man straddling a child's hobby horse and roaring with laughter. He had rarely even smiled, much less laughed.

Then she remembered the time when friends and colleagues had gathered to congratulate Joaquim on his promotion at the Rent Board. The house had been overflowing with people. Vanda was a young girl, just starting to flirt with boys. The one who had been ready to burst with happiness that day was Otacília in the midst of the group in the living room. There had been speeches and beer, and a penholder had been presented to the worthy functionary. Otacília had looked as though she were the one being honored. Joaquim had listened to the speeches, shaken all the outstretched hands, and taken the penholder unenthusiastically, as though bored by all the fuss and without the courage to say so.

Vanda remembered the expression on her father's face when she had told him that Leonardo was on his way over to ask for her hand. He had shaken his head and murmured: "Poor devil."

Vanda would not stand for any criticism of her sweetheart. "Why on earth do you call him a poor devil? He comes from a good family, he has a good job, he doesn't drink or run around. . . ."

"I know, I know. . . . I was thinking about something else."

It was odd: she could not recall many incidents connected with her father. It was as though he had never been an active participant in their life at home. She could have spent hours remembering Otacília: scenes, phrases, events in which her mother had taken part. The truth of it was that Joaquim had only begun to influence their lives on that unbelievable day when, after dubbing Leonardo "a silly ass," he had stared hard at her and Otacília and flung in their faces all at once the incredible word "Vipers!" Then, with the greatest calm in the world, as though performing an everyday act of no importance, he had gone away and never come back.

Vanda preferred not to think about that. She tried to remember her childhood, when Joaquim seemed to stand out most clearly. There was the time, for instance, when she was a curly-headed, whimpering five-year-old, that she had had that alarmingly high fever. Joaquim would not leave the room, but sat next to the little sick girl's bed, holding her hand and giving her her medicine. He had been a good father and a good husband. At that last recollection, Vanda felt more than a little touched, and—if there had been anyone else in the room—even able to cry a little, as a good daughter should.

She gazed at the body, a melancholy look on her face. His shoes shone in the candlelight, his trousers had a neat, permanent crease, his black suit-jacket fitted him perfectly, and his hands were crossed devoutly on his chest. As her eyes came to rest on his clean-shaven face, Vanda had her first shock.

She saw his smile: his cynical, immoral, mocking smile. The smile hadn't changed, and there was nothing the morticians had been able to do about it. But then, she had forgotten to make a point of asking them to give him an expression more in character, more in harmony with the solemnity of death. Quincas Wateryell's smile would endure, and in the face of that smile of mockery and amusement, what good would it do to put new shoes on him—brand new, while poor Leonardo would have to have his old ones half-soled for the second time—and what good were the black suit, the white shirt, the clean-shaved face, the slicked-down hair, the hands clasped in prayer? Quincas was making fun of it all, and his laughter was growing; in another minute it would echo through the sordid room. He laughed with his lips and his eyes, looking in the direction of the heap of dirty, patched garments left in a corner by the undertakers. It was Quincas Wateryell's smile.

And then, each syllable enunciated with insulting distinctness in the funereal silence, Vanda heard: "Viper!"

Vanda was frightened. Her eyes blazed like Otacília's, but her face turned white. That was the word he had used, almost spitting it out, when, at the very beginning of his madness, she and Otacília had tried to induce him to return to the comfort of his home, his old habits, and his lost decency. Even now, dead and stretched out in a coffin, dressed in good clothes with candles at his feet, he would not give up. He laughed with his lips and with his eyes; she would not have been surprised if he had started to whistle. And one of his thumbs—the left one—instead of being folded decorously over the other one, was sticking straight up in the air, mocking and rebellious.

"Viper!" he exclaimed again, and whistled a few mischievous notes.

Vanda gave a start and wiped her forehead with her hand. She wondered whether she was going mad. Suddenly the room seemed stifling, the heat intolerable; her head whirled. There was a huffing and puffing on the staircase: Aunt Marocas, her ample flesh quivering with exertion, entered the room. She saw her niece pale and ill in her chair, her eyes fixed on the dead man's mouth.

"You feeling faint, honey? No wonder, it's so hot in this cubbyhole."

Quincas's rascally smile broadened when he spied his sister's monumental bulk. Vanda covered her ears, knowing from experience what words he loved to use to describe Marocas. But you can't shut out a dead man's voice by putting your hands over your ears. She heard: "Sackful of shit!"

Marocas, almost recovered from the climb, opened the window wide without so much as a glance at the corpse.

"Did they pour perfume on him, or what? The smell is enough to make you dizzy."

The lively, mingled sounds of the street rushed

through the open window. The sea breeze blew out the candles and caressed Quincas's face, and the day's brightness swept over him, sky-blue and festive. Quincas settled himself more comfortably in the coffin, a triumphant smile on his lips.

VII

By this time the news of Quincas Wateryell's sudden demise was making the rounds of Bahia. True, the owners of the little shops in the Trade Mart did not shut their doors as a sign of mourning. On the other hand, they immediately raised the prices of the charm bracelets, straw purses, and clay figurines that were sold to tourists, thus paying tribute to the dead man in their own way. There were hasty, spontaneous gatherings in the vicinity of the marketplace; people walked to and fro in agitation; the news was in the air. It rode up in the Lacerda Elevator, boarded the streetcars to Calçada, and traveled in buses to Feira de Santana. Pretty black Paula cried her heart out over her tray of tapioca pancakes. Wateryell wouldn't be showing up that afternoon to shower her with gallant, well-turned phrases, trying to catch a glimpse of her large breasts and making indecent proposals that made her laugh.

In the fishing boats with their furled sails, the bronzed sailors, loyal subjects of the water goddess

Iemanjá, could not hide their dismay. How could Quincas have died like a landlubber in a stuffy room on Tabuão Street? How could the old salt give up the ghost lying tamely in bed? Hadn't Quincas Wateryell repeated over and over, with a voice and manner emphatic enough to convince even the most skeptical, that he would never die on dry land, that he was too tough and ornery for any kind of a grave but one: the sea washed in moonlight, the endless ocean?

Whenever Quincas had found himself installed as the guest of honor in the stern of a fishing boat, listening to the strumming of guitars, with the fragrant aroma of a sensational fish stew wafting up from the earthenware cooking pot while the rum bottle passed from hand to hand, there was always a certain moment when his seafaring instincts would awaken. He would rise uncertainly to his feet, the rum lending him that weaving equilibrium proper to men of the sea, and proclaim his rank as "an old sea dog." He might be an old sailor without a ship or an ocean to sail it on—a demoralized landlubber—but that was no fault of his. He had been born for a life at sea; born to hoist sails and man the tiller and best the waves on a stormy night. His destiny had been cruelly cut short; otherwise, wearing a blue uniform and smoking a pipe, he might have commanded a great ship. Anyway, he was a sailor at heart. His own mother, Madalena, had been a captain's granddaughter. He had inherited the love of the sea from his great-grandfather, and if they would let him take command of that fishing boat, he'd set sail then and there—not for nearby Maragogipe or Cachoeira, but for the far-off coast of Africa. He had never navigated before in his life, but he'd get there all right. It was in his blood. He didn't need to learn anything about sailing a ship; he had been born knowing how. If anyone in that select audience had any doubts, just let him say so. . . . He would drain the bottle in great gulps. The fishermen never doubted his word; what he said might very well be true. Kids who grew up on the docks were born knowing about the sea; it was no use trying to explain such mysteries.

On one such occasion Quincas Wateryell had taken a solemn oath: the sea would be the only witness to his final hour. He was not about to be stuck in a six-foot hole in the ground; oh no, not he! When his time came, he wanted the freedom of the seas; the voyages he hadn't been able to take when he was alive; the longest, most dangerous crossings; the most daring adventures. Cap'n Manuel, bravest of the fishing-boat captains, who had no nerves and was ageless, had nodded his head approvingly. The others, to whom life had taught that it was best not to ask too many questions, had agreed with him and taken another swallow of white rum. Tunes plucked out on the guitars had told of the magic of nights at sea and

HE WOULD RISE UNCERTAINLY
TO HIS FEET . . . AND PROCLAIM
HIS RANK AS "AN OLD SEA DOG."

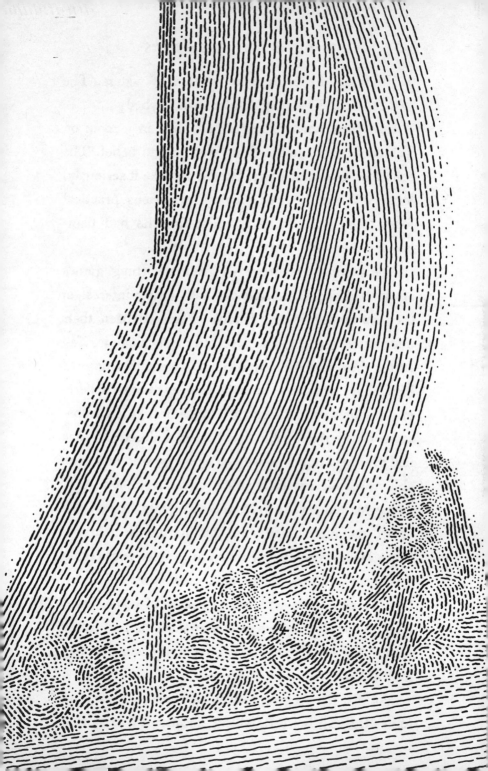

of the fatal lure of Janaína, mother of waters. The "old sea dog" had sung louder than anybody.

How then, could Quincas have died in a room on Tabuão Street? Such a thing was beyond belief. The fishermen heard the news, but did not take it seriously. Wateryell was fond of playing mysterious practical jokes; this wouldn't be the first time he had bamboozled them all.

The cardplayers broke off their absorbing games of skinball and seven and one half, losing interest in their gains and losses. Hadn't Wateryell been their undisputed leader? The late afternoon shadows fell across them like deep mourning. Melancholy reigned in the bars, the cafés, and the grocery stores—wherever liquor was sold—and if anyone drank, it was because of the irreparable loss he had suffered. No one had ever held liquor so well as Quincas, who had been able to drink an astonishing amount without ever losing his temper. In fact, the more rum he had put away, the more lucid and scintillating he had become. He had been better than anyone else at guessing the brand and provenance of a wide variety of rums, familiar as he was with every nuance of color, taste, and aroma. How long had it been since he had tasted water? Not since that unforgettable day when he had first become known as Wateryell.

Not that the occurrence was noteworthy or exciting in itself. But it is worth telling, because it was on that long-ago day that the nickname "Wateryell" became part of Quincas's name for good. He had entered a small store on the edge of the marketplace which was run by an affable Spaniard named López. A habitual customer, Quincas had long before earned the privilege of helping himself. Catching sight of a bottle on the counter, filled to the brim with clear, transparent, beautiful white rum, he poured himself out a glassful, spat to rinse out his mouth, and drank it down in a single gulp. The next instant, an inhuman bellow rent the placid morning stillness of the marketplace, shaking the very Elevator to its foundations. It was the howl of a mortally wounded animal, the cry of a man disgraced and betrayed: "Waaaaaaaaaaater!"

Oh, the dirty, filthy, lousy Spaniard! People came running from all directions, thinking someone was being murdered at the very least, while the other customers in the store roared with laughter. Quincas's "wateryell," already an anecdote, spread quickly from the marketplace to the Pillory, from the Square of the Seven Doors to the Dike, from the Calçada to Itapoã. Quincas Wateryell he was from that day on. Even Wide-Eyed Quitéria would murmur "little old Wateryell" at the tenderest moments, between love bites.

In the shacks where the lowest prostitutes lived, where tramps and loafers, petty smugglers and sailors in port found a home, family, and love late at night

IT WAS THE HOWL OF A MORTALLY
WOUNDED ANIMAL, THE CRY OF A MAN
DISGRACED AND BETRAYED. . . .

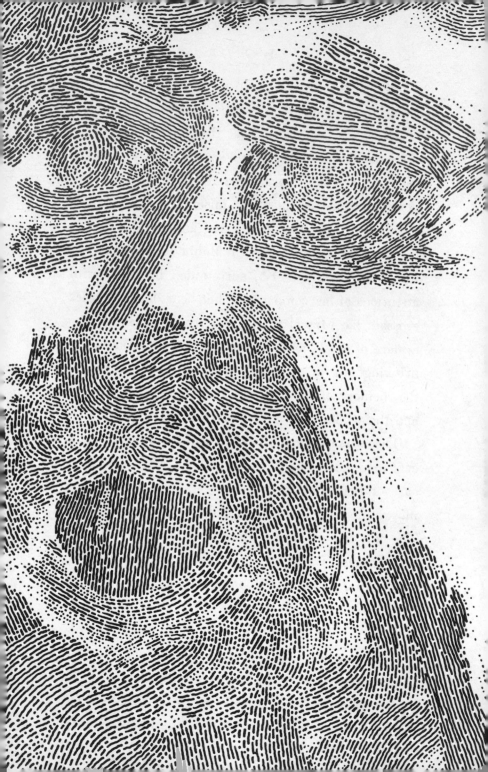

after the dreary buying and selling of sex, when the tired women longed for a little tenderness, the news of Quincas's death struck at their hearts and made them shed tears of sincere sorrow. They wept as though they had lost a close relative, and felt suddenly unprotected in their misery. Some of them counted up what they had saved and decided to buy the most beautiful flowers in Bahia for Quincas. As for Wide-Eyed Quitéria, surrounded by the tearful attentions of her companions, her heartbreaking cries crossed São Miguel Street and reached clear to the Square of the Pillory. She found some consolation in drinking and in extolling, between sobs and gulps, the memory of that incomparable lover, the fondest and the wildest, the gayest and the wisest.

The women recalled other details, phrases, and acts in praise of Quincas. It was he who had taken care of Benedita's three-month-old baby boy for almost a month when she had had to go to the hospital. The only thing he hadn't done for that baby was give it the breast. He had done everything else: changed its diapers, wiped it off, bathed it, and given it its bottle.

And hadn't he leaped to Clara Boa's defense just a few days before like a fearless champion, old and drunk as he was, when two young blades, sons of bitches from the best families in town, had tried to whip her during an orgy at Viviana's place? And

what an agreeable guest he had always been at the
noonday meal around the big table in the dining
room! There was no one else who could tell such
funny stories, or who was so good at soothing the
pangs of love, or who could take the part of a father
or an elder brother the way Quincas could.

When the afternoon was half over, Wide-Eyed
Quitéria rolled off her chair, was put to bed, and
dozed off with her memories. Several of the women
decided not to go out or have anything to do with
men that night. They were in mourning, just as
though it were Holy Thursday or Good Friday.

VIII

At sundown, when lights were going on in the city and men were leaving work, Quincas's four best friends—Curió, the Negro Bangs, Breezy, and Private Martim—descended Tabuão Street on their way to pay their respects to Quincas. It must be stated, in the interests of strict truth, that they were still sober. They had had a few drinks, no doubt, in their distress after hearing the bad news; but if their eyes were red, that was because of the tears they had shed and their infinite sorrow. How could a man be expected to stay sober when he had just lost an old friend like Quincas, the best of companions, the most thorough-going rascal in Bahia? As for the bottle that Private Martim may have carried concealed under his shirt, nothing was ever proved one way or the other.

At that dim, mysterious hour between dark and daylight, the dead man looked a little tired, Vanda thought. Well, it was no great wonder: he had spent the whole afternoon laughing, mouthing obscenities in a low voice, and making faces at her. Not even when Leonardo and Uncle Eduardo arrived, at about

five o'clock, did Quincas call a halt. He insulted
Leonardo with mutters of "nincompoop" and jeered
at Eduardo. But when the shadows of dusk settled
over the city, Quincas became restless, as though
waiting for something to happen. Vanda, in an effort
to delude herself and forget what she had seen and
heard that afternoon, carried on a lively conversation
with her husband and relatives, avoiding the dead
man's gaze. What she really wanted was to go home
and take a sleeping pill. . . . Why did Quincas's eyes
turn now to the window, now to the door?

The news had not reached all four friends at the
same time. First to hear was Curió, who employed his
multiple talents for slim wages as a store barker in
Shoemaker's Hollow. Wearing a threadbare cutaway
coat and a clown's makeup, he would take his stand
in the doorway of one of the shops and praise its high-
class goods and its low prices, stopping the passersby
with coarse jokes, urging prospective customers to
enter the shop, and practically dragging the more re-
luctant ones in by main force. From time to time,
when he felt a thirst coming over him—what a hell
of a job for drying out your chest and your gullet!—
he would step into the nearest bar for a quick one to
get his voice back in shape. It was on one of these
excursions that the bad news caught up with him, as
brutal as a sock in the jaw. He was left utterly speech-
less. He walked back in a daze and told the Syrian

. . . QUINCAS'S FOUR BEST FRIENDS . . .
DESCENDED TABUÃO STREET ON THEIR WAY
TO PAY THEIR RESPECTS TO QUINCAS.

at the shop not to count on him for the rest of the day. Curió was still young, and joy and sorrow affected him deeply. He could not bear the terrible shock alone; he needed the company of his good old friends.

There was nearly always a crowd on the bank where the fishing boats were anchored, at the market on Saturday nights, in the Square of the Seven Doors, at the ritual *capoeira* leg-wrestling matches on Liberdade Road: sailors, shopkeepers, voodoo priests, wrestlers, and idlers all took part in the endless conversations, the drinking sprees, the lively card games, the moonlight fishing parties, and the orgies in the red-light districts. Quincas Wateryell had had any number of friends and admirers, but from these four he had been inseparable. They had met every day and spent every evening together for years—broke or in the money, well-fed or starving, taking turns paying for drinks, together in good times and bad. Only now did Curió realize how close the attachment had been. Quincas's death was like an amputation; it was as though he had lost a leg or an arm, or even an eye—the eye of the heart that the voodoo priestess known as the Lady, mistress of all knowledge, had talked about. All four of them should go and pay their last respects to Quincas together.

He set off in search of Bangs, who was probably to be found in the Square of the Seven Doors at that hour, trying to scrape together enough copper coins to pay for the night's rum by helping out the bookies for the numbers game. Bangs was a Negro, almost six and a half feet tall, so big and strong that he looked like a monument when he stuck out his chest. No one could handle him when his hot temper was aroused. Luckily that did not happen often, for Bangs was guileless and easygoing by nature.

Curió had made a good guess. Bangs was sitting on the curb in the Square, sobbing as though his heart were broken and clutching an almost empty bottle. Beside him, united in sorrow and in drink, an assortment of hoboes was adding their lamentations to his. It was plain to see that Bangs had already heard what had happened. He took another swig of rum, wiped away his tears, and howled in despair: "Our Daddy's dead!"

"Daddy's dead!" the chorus wailed.

The comforting bottle was passed around; tears welled up in the Negro's eyes and his suffering became more acute: "A good man's gone!"

"Good man's gone!"

From time to time a newcomer would enter the circle, wondering what all the commotion was about. Bangs would hold out the bottle, simultaneously letting out a shriek as though being stabbed: "He was a *good* man!"

"A *good* man!" would echo all the others, except for the newcomer, still waiting for an explanation of the carryings-on and the free rum.

"Ain't you got nothin' to say, damn you?" Without getting up, Bangs would stretch out his powerful arm and shake the culprit, a dangerous glint in his eyes. "Or maybe you gonna say he *warn't* a good man?"

At that point, someone would hastily explain what had happened, before matters got out of hand.

"It was Quincas Wateryell who died."

"Quincas? He was a good man," the stranger would chime in with the chorus in terrified assent.

"Bring another bottle!" Bangs would demand between sobs.

An agile street urchin would jump up and run to the nearest store. "Bangs wants another bottle!"

As word of Quincas's death spread through the city, so did the consumption of rum.

Curió observed the scene from a distance. The news had traveled faster than he had. The Negro caught sight of him, let out a bloodcurdling howl, flung his arms heavenward, and staggered to his feet.

"Curió, old pal, our Daddy's gone!"

"Daddy's gone!" the keening chorus repeated.

"Shut your fool mouths, confound you! Lemme hug my pal Curió."

Bangs wanted to follow the courteous ritual of the

people of Bahia, the poorest and the most truly civil-
ized. The chorus obediently fell silent. The tails of
Curió's cutaway coat rose in the breeze, and tears
began to run down his painted face. Three times he
and Bangs embraced, mingling their sobs. Curió
picked up the full bottle of rum and sought solace in
it. Bangs was past consoling.

"Light's done gone out!"

"Done gone out!"

"Let's find the others and go see him," proposed
Curió.

Private Martim might be found in any one of three
or four places. He was either asleep at Carmela's,
tired out from the night before, or shooting the
breeze with his friends on the landing stage, or
gambling in the marketplace. Martim had dedicated
himself exclusively to these three occupations—love,
gossip, and gambling—since receiving his Army dis-
charge fifteen years before. He had never been employed at anything else as far as anyone knew; women
and suckers gave him enough to live on. To work
after once having been garbed in the glorious uniform of a private would have seemed disgraceful to
Martim. His haughty mulatto good looks and un-
canny skill at cards, not to speak of his nimble-
fingered guitar-playing, commanded respect.

At that particular moment, he happened to be in
the marketplace exercising his talents at cards. In so

doing he was, in his simple way, contributing to the glee of several off-duty truckers and bus drivers and to the education of two street urchins just commencing their practical apprenticeship to life, and was at the same time helping a few sellers of produce spend the day's profits—all in all, a laudable undertaking. Inexplicably, one of the players seemed to lack enthusiasm for Martim's virtuosity as a banker and was muttering between his clenched teeth that "luck like that made him smell a cheating rat." Private Martim raised his innocent blue eyes and held out the pack to the rash critic, offering to let him be the banker if he wanted to and had the necessary skill. As for him, he would just as soon bet against the bank, break it, and leave the banker flat broke. And he didn't want anybody casting aspersions on his honesty. As a former military man, he was particularly sensitive to the slightest hint of doubt regarding his honor—so sensitive, in fact, that if there was any further talk of that kind, he would be obliged to give a certain party a belt in the jaw. The urchins' enthusiasm increased, and the drivers rubbed their hands in excitement. They enjoyed nothing so much as a good fight, especially when it was spontaneous and unexpected.

At that very moment, when anything could have happened, Curió and Bangs came up bearing the tragic news and the bottle, with the chorus straggling along behind. While still some distance away, they shouted to the Private: "He's dead! He's dead!"

Private Martim regarded them with a practiced eye that lingered on the bottle, making precise calculations, and remarked to the circle at large: "It must be something pretty important if they've drunk a whole bottle. Either Bangs won the sweepstakes or Curió's got himself engaged."

For Curió was an incurable romantic, subject to sudden infatuations and the victim of frequent fulminating passions. Each new "engagement" was duly commemorated, joyfully when it began, somberly and philosophically when it was broken off shortly afterward.

"Some guy musta kicked the bucket," a driver said. Private Martim pricked up his ears.

"He's dead! He's dead!"

The two friends came nearer, bent over by the weight of the terrible news. On the way from the Square to the marketplace, with stops at the embankment and Carmela's house, they had told a great many people. Why had every single one, hearing that Quincas had gone to a better world, immediately uncorked a bottle? It was no fault of the heralds of sorrow and mourning that they had met so many people along the way, or that Quincas had had so many friends and acquaintances. On that day, the whole city of Bahia had started drinking long before the usual hour, and no wonder. A Quincas Wateryell doesn't die every day in the year.

Private Martim, forgetting his quarrel and the pack of cards in his hand, observed the approaching pair with growing curiosity. They were crying, he could see that. Bangs's choked voice reached him: "Our Daddy's dead!"

"Who, Jesus Christ or the Governor?" one of the urchins asked, trying to be witty. The Negro's big hand lifted him up and flung him down. The onlookers realized now that whatever had happened, it was no laughing matter. Curió raised the bottle and cried out: "Wateryell's dead!"

The cards fell from Martim's hand, and the suspicious player saw his darkest doubts confirmed: aces and queens—banker's cards—were scattered profusely about. But Quincas's name had reached his ears, and he decided not to make trouble just then. Private Martim took the bottle from Curió, emptied it at a gulp, and threw it away contemptuously. He gazed for a long time at the marketplace, the trucks and buses in the street, the canoes out on the water, the pedestrians coming and going. He felt suddenly empty inside and deaf to the singing of the caged birds in their stall close by.

He was not the sort of man to shed tears. A military man doesn't cry, not even after he has stopped wearing his uniform. But his eyes became smaller, and his voice lost its blustering tone. It was almost a child's voice that asked: "How can he be dead?"

After he had picked up the cards, he joined the other two. They still had to find Breezy, who had no sure resting-place except on Thursday and Sunday afternoons, when he invariably took part in the *capoeira* wrestling matches with Valdemar's gang out on Liberdade Road. The rest of the time he hunted for rats and toads to sell to the laboratories to be used in medical examinations and scientific experiments, an occupation that had earned him the esteem of his friends. Wasn't he something of a scientist in his own right? Didn't he converse with doctors, and wasn't he familiar with jawbreaking words?

Only after a long trudge and a good many swigs of rum did they catch up with him, huddled up in his capacious jacket as if he were cold, mumbling to himself. He had heard the news from another source and was coming to look for his friends. When he caught sight of them, he fished in one of his pockets—to get out a handkerchief to wipe his eyes with, thought Curió. But Breezy pulled from the depths of his pocket, not a handkerchief but a little bullfrog, as shiny and green as an emerald.

"I was savin' it for Quincas. It's the prettiest one I ever found."

IX

When the four friends appeared at the door of Quincas's room, Breezy held out his extended palm, on which the little popeyed frog was perched. They stopped in the doorway, one behind the other, Bangs craning his big head forward to see better. Breezy shamefacedly put the animal back in his pocket.

The family interrupted its animated conversation, and four pairs of hostile eyes stared at the intruders. This is all we need, thought Vanda. Private Martim, who yielded the palm to none but Quincas when it came to finesse, took off his seedy hat and greeted the company: "Good evenin', ladies and gentlemen. We wanted to pay him a visit."

He took a step forward into the room, and the others followed. The family drew back, and the newcomers crowded around the coffin. At first Curió thought there must have been some mistake; that couldn't be Quincas Wateryell. He wouldn't have known him at all except for his smile. All four were taken aback; they would never have dreamed that Quincas could look so clean, so elegant, or so well-

60

dressed. Their self-assurance vanished; their recent intoxication melted away as if by magic. The presence of the family—especially that of the women—intimidated them. They didn't know how to act, what to do with their hands, or how to behave with the dead man looking on.

Curió, ridiculous with his crimson-painted face and his shiny cutaway coat, looked at his three companions pleadingly. He wanted to get out of that room, the quicker the better. Private Martim wavered for a moment, like a general calculating the enemy's forces on the eve of a battle. Breezy actually took a step toward the door. Only Bangs, still a little behind the others, with his big head thrust forward, refused to hesitate for an instant. Quincas was smiling at him, and the big Negro smiled back. No human being on earth could have dragged him away, now that he was near his beloved Quincas. He grasped Breezy by the arm and answered Curió's mute appeal with a look of scorn. Private Martim understood: a soldier never runs away from the battlefield. The four withdrew from the coffin to the back of the room.

Silence fell between Joaquim Soares da Cunha's family, on one side, and Quincas Wateryell's friends, on the other. Breezy put his hand in his pocket and touched the frightened bullfrog. How he did long to show it to Quincas!

As though performing a ballet step, the relatives

. . . THE FOUR FRIENDS APPEARED
AT THE DOOR OF QUINCAS'S ROOM. . . .

approached the coffin as the friends drew back. Vanda flung at her father a glance full of scornful reproach. Even now that he was dead, he still preferred the society of those ragamuffins. They were the ones that Quincas had been waiting for. His late afternoon restlessness had had only one cause: the long time it had taken those bums to get there. Just when Vanda had thought her father defeated; just when he finally seemed ready to give in and shut his filthy mouth, vanquished by the silent, dignified resistance with which she had defied his many provocations, there was that smile again on the dead face. The corpse before her was, more than ever, Quincas Wateryell. If it had not been for the thought of Otacília's outraged memory, she would have given up the struggle, left his undeserving body just where it was, returned the practically new casket to the undertakers, and sold the new clothes at half price to the first peddler she saw. The silence was becoming intolerable.

Leonardo turned to his wife and her aunt: "I think you'd better go on now. It's getting late."

Only a few minutes earlier, Vanda's one desire had been to go home and rest. She gritted her teeth; she wasn't the kind of woman to give in without a fight: "In a little while."

Bangs sat down on the floor and rested his head against the wall. Breezy nudged him with his foot;

it didn't look right to make himself comfortable like that in front of Quinca's family. Curió still wanted to beat a retreat; Private Martim looked at the Negro reproachfully. Pushing his friend's bothersome foot away, Bangs let out a sob: "He was jest like a Daddy to us! Poor old Daddy Quincas."

Vanda felt as though she had been struck; Leonardo, as though he had been slapped; Eduardo, as though he had been spat at. Only Aunt Marocas laughed, her fat sides shaking on the single disputed chair: "How funny!"

Bangs, charmed with Marocas, switched abruptly from tears to laughter. The Negro's booming guffaw, resounding like a thunderclap in the little room, was even more frightful than his loud sobs. Worst of all, Vanda distinctly heard another laugh along with Bangs's: Quincas was enjoying himself hugely.

"What do you mean by such a lack of proper respect?" Her dry voice cut short the budding cordiality.

Chastened by the reprimand, Aunt Marocas got up and walked about the room, closely followed by Bangs's friendly gaze as he inspected her from head to foot. He was finding her quite to his taste—a little past her prime, no doubt about that, but nice and fat, just the kind of woman he liked. He had no use at all for those pale, skinny ones; you couldn't even give their waists a good, hard squeeze. If Bangs ever ran into this old girl on the beach, what they wouldn't do! You could tell she was the right kind just by looking at her. Marocas, who was beginning to feel tired and nervous, said she wanted to go home. Vanda, having taken her place in the chair next to the casket, did not reply. She might have been jealously guarding a treasure.

"We're all tired," Eduardo said.

"It's time they started home." Leonardo was afraid of what Tabuão Street would be like later on, when all the stores were locked up for the night and the prostitutes and idlers took over.

Naturally courteous and wanting to be helpful, Private Martim made a suggestion: "If the gentlemen want to go take a nap, we'll stay here and mind Quincas."

Eduardo knew that wasn't right; they couldn't leave the body alone with those people, without a single member of the family to stand watch. But oh, how he longed to do exactly that! A whole day in the store, running back and forth waiting on the customers and giving orders to those stupid clerks, was enough to wear a man out. Eduardo always went to bed early and woke up at dawn; his timetable was inflexible. Every evening when he got back from the store he would take a bath, have dinner, sit down in his easy chair, stretch out his legs, and fall asleep. That brother of his had never given him anything but trouble. In fact, Quincas had done nothing but make trouble for the past ten years. And here he was tonight, still up at this ungodly hour after having eaten nothing but a couple of sandwiches. After all, why shouldn't they leave him alone with his friends, or rather that gang of hoboes he had been hanging around with all these years? What were they doing in that filthy rat's nest, anyway—he and Marocas, Vanda and Leonardo? He was not quite brave enough to say what he was thinking: Vanda had no tact and was quite capable of reminding him of various occasions when he, Eduardo, just starting out in business, had touched Quincas for a loan. He looked at Private Martim with some benevolence.

Breezy, whose attempts to make Bangs get up had all met with failure, sat down. He was itching to put the bullfrog in the palm of his hand and play with it. It was the prettiest one he had ever seen, by a long shot. Curió, who had spent part of his childhood in an orphanage run by priests, ransacked his rusty memory for a suitable prayer. He had always heard that dead people had to have prayers. Priests, too. . . . Had the priest already been there, or would he come the next morning? The question tickled his throat and he could not refrain from asking: "Did the priest come?"

"Tomorrow morning," Marocas replied.

Vanda shot her a look of reproach. Why did she insist on talking to those unsavory characters? But now that a proper atmosphere of respect had been re-established, Vanda felt better. She had banished the tramps to a corner of the room and reduced them to silence. After all, she and Aunt Marocas could not very well spend the night there. She had had a vague hope, in the beginning, that Quincas's indecent friends would not stay very long, nothing to eat or drink having been offered. She could not understand why they were still in the room at all. It wasn't out of friendship for the dead man, certainly; that sort of people didn't know what friendship was. Be that as it might, even the annoying presence of such friends as these made no difference, as long as they didn't join the funeral procession the next day. When they all came back for the funeral in the morning, she, Vanda, would take charge. The family would be alone with the corpse, and she would see to it that Joaquim Soares da Cunha was buried in a modest, dignified way. She rose from her chair, said "Come on" to Marocas, and turned to Leonardo: "Don't stay much longer. You can't afford to lose a night's sleep. Uncle Eduardo's already offered to spend the night."

Eduardo nodded and took possession of the vacated chair, and Leonardo got up to accompany the two women to the streetcar. Private Martim ventured a "Good night, ladies," and got no answer for his pains. The only light in the room came from the flickering candles. Bangs snored menacingly in his sleep.

X

At ten o'clock Leonardo, getting up painfully from the kerosene drum, went over to the candles to see the time. He awakened Eduardo, who was dozing uncomfortably in the chair with his mouth open: "I'm going home now. I'll be back tomorrow at six to give you time to go home and change."

Eduardo stretched his legs and thought about bed. He had a crick in his neck. Curió, Breezy, and Private Martim were carrying on a fascinating argument in the corner, trying to settle which of them was to take Quincas's place in the heart and bed of Wide-Eyed Quitéria. Private Martim, in a disgusting display of self-interest, refused to be crossed off the list of those eligible, even though he already rejoiced in the possession of the slim body and affectionate heart of the pretty Negress Carmela.

Eduardo stared at the group as the echo of Leonardo's steps died away down the street. The argument stopped, and Private Martim smiled at the shopowner, who looked enviously at the peacefully sleeping Bangs. He settled himself in the chair and put his feet up on the kerosene drum. He still had a crick in his neck.

Breezy could not resist taking the frog out of his pocket and putting it on the ground. The funny little thing hopped about amusingly, like a mischievous spirit let loose in the room. Eduardo could not get to sleep. He glanced resentfully at the dead man lying motionless in his coffin, the only person there who was comfortable. What the devil was he, Eduardo, doing there, anyway? Wasn't it enough that he was going to the funeral and paying part of the expenses? He had done more than his duty as a brother already, when you stopped to think about what kind of brother Quincas had been—a scandal and a pest. He stood up, stretched his arms and legs, and gave a wide yawn. Breezy hid the little green frog in his hand. Curió thought about Wide-Eyed Quitéria . . . a woman and then some. Eduardo stopped in front of them.

"Let me ask you something."

Private Martim, an expert psychologist by vocation and necessity, stood at attention: "At your service, Commander."

You never could tell. Maybe the merchant would have a nip of something brought in to help them get through the long night.

"Are you all planning to spend the night?"

"With Quincas? Yessir. We're friends of his."

"Then I'll go home and sleep for a while." He put his hand in his pocket and took out a bill, every movement accompanied by the eager gaze of Curió, Breezy, and the Private. "Here you are—go buy yourselves some sandwiches. But make sure you don't leave him alone for a minute, understand?"

"Don't you worry none; we'll keep him company."

Bangs woke up when he smelled the rum. Before getting down to the serious business of drinking, Curió and Breezy took out cigarettes and Private Martim lit up one of those strong, black fifty-centavo cigars that only real connoisseurs can appreciate. He waved the reeking weed under the Negro's nose, but even that didn't wake him. However, they had no sooner uncorked the bottle (that quasi-mythical bottle that, according to Quincas's family, the Private had brought in under his shirt) than the Negro opened his eyes and demanded his fair share.

The first few drinks aroused in the four friends a marked tendency to criticize. You'd have to go a mighty long way to find a stingier bunch than those stuck-up folks of Quincas who thought so much of themselves. They had done everything by halves. Where were the chairs for the company to sit on? Where were the food and drinks that were always served, even at poor people's wakes? Private Martim had been to a good many death vigils, but he had never seen one as dead as this. Even at the poorest wakes, guests were offered a cup of coffee and a swallow of rum, at least. Quincas deserved better treatment than this. A lot of good it did for his people to go around bragging about their own importance, and then turn around and humiliate a dead man by not offering his friends anything to eat or drink!

Breezy and Curió went in search of chairs and provisions: Private Martim thought that someone should organize things with a minimum of decency. Enthroned on the chair, he gave orders for boxes and bottles. Bangs, occupying the kerosene drum, assented with an approving nod.

They had to admit that as far as the corpse was concerned, the family had done itself proud. Quincas had a new suit and new shoes and looked elegant. And those were nice candles, too; pretty enough for a church. But even here the family had skimped: they had forgotten the flowers. Who had ever heard of a corpse without flowers?

"Son of a gun!" Bangs exploded. "He sure does make a fine-lookin' corpse."

Quincas smiled at the praise, and the Negro smiled back at him. "That's right, Daddy," he said, and poked him in the ribs as he always had when Quincas told a good one.

Breezy and Curió returned with a couple of crates, a hunk of salami, and several bottles of rum. When they had arranged themselves in a semicircle around the dead man, Curió proposed that they repeat the Lord's Prayer in unison. In a remarkable feat of memory, he had managed to remember practically all of it. The others agreed unenthusiastically; they knew it wouldn't be easy. Bangs knew a few invocations to the voodoo gods Oxum and Oxalá, but that was as far as his knowledge of religion went. Breezy hadn't said a prayer in thirty years. Private Martim considered prayers and church-going weaknesses unbefitting a military man. Even so, they tried their best, Curió beginning each phrase and the others straggling along as best they could. Finally Curió (who had knelt down and bowed his head in a posture of contrition) lost patience and exclaimed angrily: "Well, if you ain't a bunch of thick-headed fools!"

"We're out of practice," the Private explained. "Anyway, it's better than nothin'. The padre can finish the job tomorrow."

Quincas listened indifferently to the praying. He was probably uncomfortable in those hot clothes, anyway. Bangs scrutinized his friend, thinking that they ought to do something else to entertain him, the prayer not having come out right. Maybe they should sing a few vodoo chants. They had to do something. He turned to Breezy.

"Where's the toad? Let's give it to him."

"It ain't a toad, it's a bullfrog. Ain't no use to him now."

"Maybe he'd like it anyway."

Breezy picked up the frog and set it delicately between Quincas's clasped hands. The little animal
hopped into the depths of the coffin; coruscating
green flashes ran up and down the corpse in the
wavering candlelight.

Private Martim and Curió resumed their argument about Wide-Eyed Quitéria. Drink had made
Curió more aggressive; he raised his voice in defense
of his own interests. Bangs expostulated: "Ain't you
ashamed, fightin' over his girl right in front of him?
He ain't even cold yet and you all come crowdin'
around like vultures sniffin' fresh meat."

"He can decide himself," Breezy ruled. He was in
hopes of being chosen by Quincas to inherit Quitéria,
his only possession. After all, hádn't he brought him
the prettiest little green bullfrog he had ever caught?

"Humph!" the corpse said.

"You hear? He don't like that kind of talk," the
Negro cried angrily.

"Let's give him a swig, too," the Private suggested,
eager to get into Quincas's good graces.

They opened his mouth and poured in a shot of
rum, some of which spilled over his collar and down
his shirtfront.

"No wonder. Who ever heard of tryin' to drink
lyin' down?"

"Let's set him up so he can see us."

They adjusted Quincas to a sitting position in the coffin. His head bobbed from one side to the other, and after the swig of rum, his smile grew broader.

"This here's a fine jacket," Private Martim said, examining the material. "There ain't no sense in puttin' brand new clothes on a corpse. When you're dead you're dead; you go down under the ground, and that's all there is to it. It just ain't right, givin' new clothes to the worms to eat, when there's plenty of folks walkin' around that could use 'em."

How true that was, they thought, giving another drink to Quincas, who nodded in agreement. The sort of man who supported truth from whatever quarter it came, he was evidently in full accord with Martim's reasoning.

"He's gonna ruin his clothes."

"Let's take off his coat so he won't mess it up."

Quincas looked relieved when the heavy, hot, black jacket had been removed. Because he still spat out rum with every swallow he took, they removed his shirt as well. Curió had taken a fancy to the shiny shoes; his own were coming to pieces. What did a dead man want with shoes anyway, eh, Quincas?

"They're just my size."

Bangs retrieved his friend's old clothes from the corner. After they had dressed him in them, he was recognizable once more.

"Now it's old Quincas again!"

They were all in better spirits by this time. Quincas himself looked more cheerful, now that he had been relieved of the uncomfortable new garments. He was particularly grateful to Curió—the shoes had been pinching his feet. The barker seized this momentary advantage to put his mouth close to Quincas's ear and whisper something about Quitéria. Why had he done it? Bangs had been right when he had warned that Quincas wouldn't stand for any talk about the girl. He flared up violently and spat a mouthful of rum in Curió's eye. The others shivered with fright.

"He got mad."

"I told you he would!"

Breezy had put on the new trousers, Private Martim had appropriated the jacket, and Bangs had kept the shirt to swap for a bottle of rum in a bar where he was well known. They lamented the omission of shorts. As tactfully as possible, Private Martim said to Quincas: "Maybe it ain't polite to say so, but that family of yours ain't what I'd call big spenders. I guess your son-in-law swiped the shorts."

Quincas was more direct. "Cheapskates, every last one of them."

"Well, seein' as how you said it yourself, it's the plain truth. We didn't want to say so; after all, they're your relatives. But what stingy pikers! Who ever heard of a wake where the folks that came had to buy their own drinks?"

"An' not a single flower," Bangs put in. "Relatives like that I can do without."

"The men are jackasses and the women are vipers," Quincas remarked bluntly.

"Listen, Daddy, that chubby one ain't so bad. She got a real sweet backside."

"A sackful of shit, that's what she is."

"Now, Daddy, don't you talk that way. Maybe she ain't quite what she used to be, but she ain't as bad as that. I've seen worse."

"You dumb nigger, you don't know a good-looking dame when you see one."

Breezy, with no sense at all of what was fitting, spoke up: "Quitéria's the one who's good-lookin', ain't she, Quincas? What you reckon she's gonna do now? I was thinkin' maybe—"

"Shut up, damn you! You want him to get mad again?"

Quincas was not even listening. Turning to Private Martim, who had quietly skipped him when serving the last round of drinks, he almost knocked the bottle out of the Private's hand with his head.

"Give Daddy his share," Bangs demanded.

"But he was wastin' it," the Private objected.

"You let him drink it any way he wants to. He got a right to, ain't he?"

Private Martim thrust the rim of the bottle into Quincas's open mouth. "Take it easy, old pal, I wasn't tryin' to do you out of nothin'. Go on and drink up. After all, it's your party."

They had tacitly agreed to drop the argument about Quitéria; obviously Quincas would tolerate no reference to the matter.

"Good rum!" Curió said.

"Lousy!" Quincas the connoisseur corrected.

"Well, after all, at that price. . . ."

The bullfrog hopped onto Quincas's chest. He looked at it admiringly and stowed it away in the pocket of his greasy old coat.

The moon of Bahia, showering silver light over the city and the bay, looked in through the window. The sea breeze came with it and blew out the candles; the coffin disappeared in the darkness. Guitar music filled the street, blending with a woman's voice singing a plaintive love song. Private Martim began to sing too.

"Quincas loves a good tune."

The four sang in harmony, Bangs's deep bass rumbling beyond the hill and out to where the fishing boats were anchored. They drank and sang, and Quincas, who loved a good tune, did not miss a drink or a note. When they had sung their fill, Curió asked suddenly: "Ain't Cap'n Manuel's fish fry tonight?"

"Sure is. And the fish is ray," Breezy answered emphatically.

"Ain't nobody can make a fish stew as good as Maria Clara," the Private declared.

Quincas smacked his lips, and Bangs laughed.

"He's crazy about fish stew."

"Well, why don't we go? Cap'n Manuel's feelin's might be hurt if we don't."

They eyed one another. It was already getting late; they would still have to pick up the women. Curió expressed his doubts: "We promised not to leave him alone."

"Who's gonna leave him alone? He's comin' with us."

"I'm hungry," Bangs said.

They consulted Quincas: "You want to go?"

"Why shouldn't I go? Do I look like I'm crippled?"

One more gulp and they had emptied the bottle. They set Quincas on his feet. Bangs remarked: "Can't even stand up, he's so drunk. He's gettin' older; can't hold his liquor like he used to. Come on, Daddy, let's go."

Curió and Breezy took the lead. Quincas pranced along arm in arm with Bangs and Private Martim, as happy as a king.

XI

It looked as though it would be a night to remember. Quincas Wateryell was in splendid form. An unwonted enthusiasm took possession of the little group, making them feel as though that wonderful night, with the light of a full moon enveloping the mystery of Bahia, belonged to them alone. On the Street of the Pillory, couples hid in doorways that were centuries old; cats meowed on the rooftops; guitars played mournful serenades. It was a night of enchantment. Drumbeats throbbed in the distance, and Pillory Square resembled a fantastic stageset.

Quincas Wateryell was enjoying himself to the hilt. He tried to trip up Martim and the Negro, stuck out his tongue at passersby, put his head into a doorway to peer maliciously at a couple of lovers, and threatened to fall flat in the street at every step. The five friends were no longer in any hurry. It was as if time itself belonged to them, as if they had gone beyond the calendar and could make that magic night in Bahia go on for a week. For, as Bangs solemnly declared, Quincas Wateryell's birthday could hardly be celebrated properly in the space of a few short hours. Quincas did not deny that it was his birthday, although the others could not remember ever having celebrated it before. What they had celebrated had been Curió's countless engagements, Maria Clara's and Quitéria's birthdays, and, on one occasion, a scientific discovery made by one of Breezy's customers, when the elated scientist had pressed a 500-milreis note into the hand of his "humble colleague." But they were celebrating Quincas's birthday for the first time, and they had to celebrate it right. They walked up Pillory Hill to Quitéria's house.

It struck them as odd that none of the usual racket was coming from the bars and the women's houses in São Miguel Street. Everything was different that night. Had there been an unexpected police raid? Had the inspectors closed the establishments and shuttered up the bars? Had they dragged off Quitéria, Carmela, Doralice, Ernestina, and fat Margarida? Were they about to fall into a trap? Private Martim took command of the operation: Curió was chosen to spy out the land.

"You be the pathfinder," the Private ordered.

They sat down on the church steps to wait for him; there was still one last bottle to finish up. Quincas lay on his back, looking up at the sky and smiling in the moonlight.

Curió returned in the midst of a shouting, cheer-

THE FIVE FRIENDS
WERE NO LONGER IN ANY HURRY.

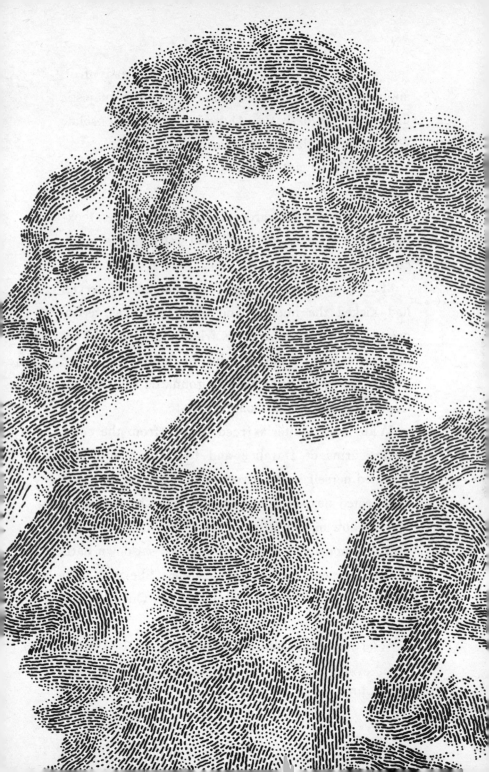

ing group. Easily recognizable at the head of it, supported by two other women, was the majestic figure of Wide-Eyed Quitéria, the disconsolate widow, all in black and wearing a mantilla.

"Where's he at? Where's he at?" she yelled excitedly.

Curió hurried forward and ran up the steps, looking like a speaker at a political rally in his shiny cutaway.

"Folks, the news was goin' around that Wateryell had kicked the bucket, and everybody was feelin' pretty bad." Quincas and his friends laughed. "Well, he's right here, folks, it's his birthday, and we're givin' a party for him. There's gonna be fish stew on Cap'n Manuel's fishin' boat!"

Wide-Eyed Quitéria freed herself from the comforting arms of Doralice and fat Margô and precipitated herself in the direction of Quincas, who was now seated next to Bangs on the church steps. But Quitéria, owing doubtless to the deep emotion of that supreme moment, lost her balance and sat down hard on her rear end on the cobblestones. She was soon helped to her feet and led to where Quincas was sitting.

"You no-'count, worthless man! What you mean tellin' everybody you was dead and scarin' folks half to death!"

She sat down beside the smiling Quincas, took his hand, and placed it over her heaving bosom to let him feel the palpitations of her afflicted heart.

"I like to have died when I heard, and you laughin' all the time and havin' yourself a good time, you good-for-nothin' man. What I goin' to do with you, Wateryell, you ole devil? You and your fabrications! Can't do a thing with you nohow, Wateryell. You like to have killed me. . . ."

The group walked on in the direction of Quitéria's house, their talk punctuated by bursts of loud laughter. The noise started up again in the bars; life had come back to São Miguel Street. Quitéria looked beautiful in her black dress; never had so many men desired her.

As they went along steep São Miguel Street, they were showered with one affectionate demonstration after another. At the Flower of São Miguel, Hansen the German offered a round of drinks. A little farther on, Verger the Frenchman distributed African amulets to the women. He couldn't go with them that night because he had to fulfill a vow he had made to one of the saints.

The doors of the bordellos were thrown open again, and women appeared in the windows and on the sidewalks. All along the way, people were calling out to Quincas and shouting *"Viva!"* He thanked them with courteous nods of his head to left and right, like a monarch returning in triumph to his kingdom.

In Quitéria's house all was dejection and sorrow. Over the chest of drawers in her bedroom—in the place of honor next to a print of Our Lord of Bonfim and a clay figure of Quitéria's voodoo guide, the Indian Aroeira—was enshrined a picture of Quincas cut out of a newspaper (one of a series of articles by Giovanni Guimarães on the "underworld of Bahia"), with a candle burning on either side and a red rose underneath. Doralice, who shared Quitéria's rooms, had already opened a bottle and passed around drinks in the best blue glasses. Quitéria blew out the candles, Quincas lay down on the bed, and the others retired into the parlor, where Quitéria soon joined them, saying disgustedly: "Old fool's gone to sleep."

"He was jus' too drunk to hold out," explained Breezy.

"You let him be," Bangs advised. "He jus' impossible today. You let him rest a little bit."

But they were already late for the fish fry, and the only thing to do, after waiting a few minutes, was to wake up Quincas again. Quitéria, black Carmela, and fat Margarida were going with them. Doralice had to refuse the invitation; she had just been handed a note from Dr. Carmino saying that he was coming that night. They all knew that Dr. Carmino paid by the month; it was something Doralice could count on. She couldn't very well disappoint him.

They descended the steep street, hurrying this time. Quincas was almost running; he stumbled on the cobblestones, dragging along Quitéria and Bangs who were holding on to him. They hoped to get there in time to find the fishing boat still at anchor.

They made one last stop at the bar of Cazuza, an old friend. The place was frequented by some ugly customers, including a gang of marijuana addicts; hardly a night went by without a brawl of some sort. Cazuza was a good man, though; he let them have drinks, and occasionally a whole bottle, on credit. They couldn't very well show up at the party empty-handed, so they hoped to talk Cazuza into giving them three or four bottles of the good stuff. While Private Martim, the irresistible diplomat, whispered at the bar with its owner, who was stunned at beholding Quincas Wateryell in fine fettle, the others sat down to whet their appetites with a little something on the house in honor of Quincas's birthday. The bar was full of glum youths, cheerful sailors, prostitutes on their last legs, and truck drivers about to hit the road for Feira de Santana.

The altercation, when it broke out unexpectedly, was a rip-roaring one. Apparently Quincas was really to blame. He had been sitting with his head resting on Quitéria's bosom and his legs stretched out. It

appears that one of the sullen young men, wanting
to get by, had tripped over Quincas's legs, had almost fallen, and had used abusive language, which
Bangs had resented. That night Quincas had every
privilege in the world, including the right to stick
his legs out any way he had a mind to, and Bangs
said as much. As the boy did not put up a fight,
nothing happened just then. A few minutes later,
however, another marijuana smoker wanted to get by
and asked Quincas to move his legs out of the way.
Quincas pretended not to hear him. The skinny fel-
low cursed and gave him a violent push, Quincas
returned the blow with his head, and the fight was
on. Bangs seized the young man and flung him on
top of another table—his usual method of coping
with such situations. The whole marijuana ring bore
down on him in fury, and after that it was impossible
to tell what was going on. All that could be seen
was the beautiful Quitéria, standing on a chair and
brandishing a bottle. Private Martim took command.

When the free-for-all had ended in total victory
for Quincas's friends, aided by the truck drivers,
Breezy had a black eye and one of Curió's coattails
was torn—the only real piece of damage. The marijuana addicts had fled. As for Quincas, he was
stretched out unconscious on the floor, having ab-
sorbed some violent blows and hit his head on the
tiles in the passageway.

Quitéria bent over Quincas, trying to bring him to his senses. Cazuza gazed philosophically at the wreckage of the bar, with its overturned tables and broken glassware. He was used to this sort of thing; the news would increase the fame of his bar and bring in more customers. He rather enjoyed a good fight himself.

A good stiff drink finally brought Quincas around. He still drank in that peculiar way of his, spitting out part of the rum—a real waste of good liquor. If it had not been his birthday, Private Martim would have called his attention to it tactfully. They set out for the wharf.

Cap'n Manuel had given them up by that time. The stew was getting low in the pot, having been consumed right there on the dock; Manuel wasn't about to put out to sea as long as only fishermen were gathered around the big earthenware caldron. In his heart he had not believed the news of Quincas's death for a minute, and was consequently not at all surprised to see him arrive arm in arm with Quitéria. He knew that the old sailor could never pass away in an ordinary bed, on dry land.

"There's plenty of fish for all!"

They let out the sails and pulled up the great stone that served as an anchor. The sea was a silver road in the moonlight, and behind them the city of Bahia was silhouetted against the black mountain.

. . . AFTER THAT IT WAS IMPOSSIBLE
TO TELL WHAT WAS GOING ON.

The boat glided gently away, while Maria Clara's voice rose in a sailors' song:

I found you deep down in the sea,
All dressed in shells. . . .

The steaming pot was surrounded by earthenware plates held out to be filled with fragrant fish drowned in palm oil and pepper. The bottle of white rum was passed around. Private Martim could be counted upon never to lose his clear-eyed perspective of present necessities. Even while commanding the battle, he had managed to filch a few bottles and conceal them under the women's dresses. Quincas and Quitéria were the only ones not eating: they lay in the stern of the fishing boat, half listening to Maria Clara's singing, while the beautiful wide-eyed one spoke words of love to the old sailor: "What you want to go an' scare everybody for, bad old Quincas? Don't you know I got a weak heart an' the doctor told me not to fret? Where you get such tomfool notions? An' how you think I'm gonna live without you, you devil-man? I'se used to bein' with you, an' the crazy things you says, you wicked ole man, and your funny ways, and your way of bein' good to me. Why'd you treat me so bad today?" She held his wounded head and kissed his sly eyes.

Quincas, breathing in the salt air, gave her no answer. One of his hands trailed in the water, leaving a wake behind it. All was peaceful and calm: Maria Clara's voice, the superb fish stew, the strong breeze turning into a stiff wind, the moon in the sky, and Quitéria's murmuring voice. But suddenly clouds boiled up from the south and engulfed the full moon. The stars went out, and the wind turned cold and dangerous. Cap'n Manuel warned: "There's a bad storm comin' up; we'd better go back."

He wanted to get the fishing boat back to the dock before the storm broke. But the rum was pleasant, the talk was good; there was still plenty of fish in the pot, floating in yellow palm oil, and Maria Clara's singing induced a kind of melancholy languor, a desire to linger on the water. And then, how could they interrupt the idyll of Quincas and Quitéria on that festive night?

And so the storm, with howling winds and waves lashed into whitecaps, caught them on the way. The lights of Bahia glimmered in the distance; a jagged ray of lightning slashed the darkness, and rain began to fall. Cap'n Manuel puffed on his pipe at the tiller.

No one knows to this day how Quincas got to his feet and leaned against the aftersail. Quitéria did not once take her enamored eyes off the figure of the old sailor smiling at the waves washing over the deck

. . . THEY SAW QUINCAS
THROW HIMSELF OVERBOARD. . . .

and the flashes of lightning that lit up the blackness. Men and women hung on to the ropes or clung to the rails. The wind whistled, and the little vessel threatened to capsize at any moment. Maria Clara fell silent, and went to stand next to her man at the tiller.

Waves broke over the little craft, and the wind nearly tore away the sails. The only steady things were the glow from Cap'n Manuel's pipe and the figure of Quincas erect in the midst of the storm, imperturbable and majestic—the old sailor. Slowly and painfully, the fishing boat struggled toward the calm waters inside the sea wall. Just a little while longer, and the party could begin all over again.

Just then there were five flashes of lightning, one after another. A thunderbolt reverberated as though the world were coming to an end, and a gigantic wave lifted the boat. Cries of terror burst from men and women alike, and fat Margô exclaimed: "Holy Mary preserve us!"

When the crash of the furious waves against the imperiled fishing boat was at its height and ragged streaks of lightning lit up the sky, they saw Quincas throw himself overboard and heard his last words.

The boat was already entering the calmer seas beyond the breakwater. But Quincas, wrapped in a shroud of waves and sea foam, had chosen of his own free will to remain in the storm.

XII

The undertakers refused to take back the casket, even for half its original price. The family had to pay up; but Vanda was able to use the leftover candles. The coffin is still in Eduardo's storehouse, waiting for some dead man to buy it secondhand. As for Quincas's last words, there are several different versions. But who could swear to what he had heard in the middle of a storm like that? According to a ballad singer in the market, this is what really happened:

> *In the wind and the rain*
> *They heard Quincas say:*
> *"I'll be buried when I please*
> *In my own sweet way.*
> *You can keep your coffin*
> *For another time.*
> *I ain't goin' down*
> *In a hole in the ground.*
> *'Cause I know best—"*
> *And they couldn't hear the rest.*